Mikey Goes to School

First of *The Mikey and Mommy Series*

Written and Illustrated By
Tom Racanelli

Produced By
StarWeb Publishing

www.StarWebPublishing.com

Cover Design by: Miguel A. Calderón
Illustrations Professionally Digitized by: Miguel A. Calderón

ISBN-13: 978-0998597836
ISBN-10: 099859783X

To Evie & Quinn

Dedication

This "first of a series" preschool book is dedicated to the Gluck Childcare Center in La Jolla, California and to all of the wonderful children who I have been blessed to work with there.

Two GREAT Kids!

Mr. Tom

Mikey loves Mommy very much.

It is Monday morning and Mommy will take Mikey to preschool.

Mikey had a great weekend playing with his friends and going to the beach with Mommy and Daddy.

Mommy helps Mikey get buckled into his car seat in their big blue car.

Every weekday, Mommy drives Mikey to school. She always remembers to pack his lunch and bring his water bottle too.

Sometimes he brings a toy or book to share when it's his day to share at circle time.

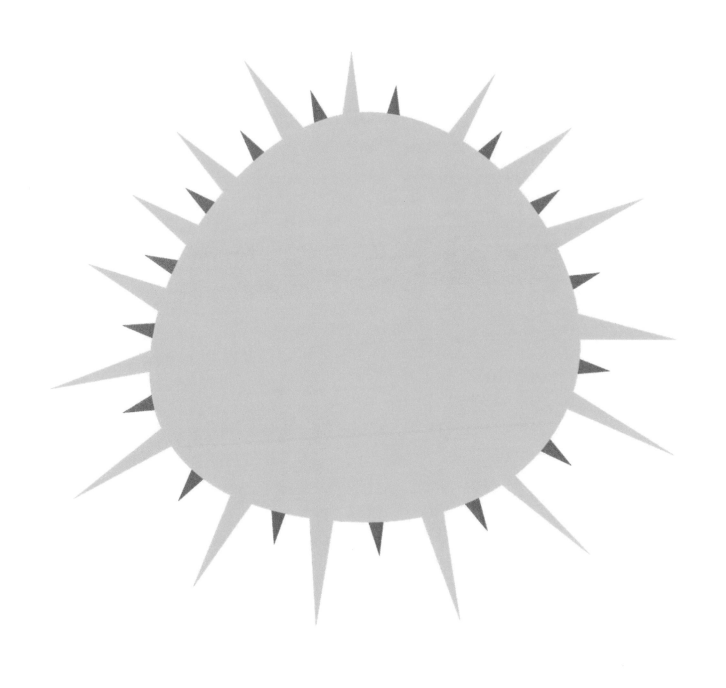

Mikey looks out the window and sees the big, bright Sun.

He knows it is going to be a warm, sunny day, and he feels the hot rays shining in through his window.

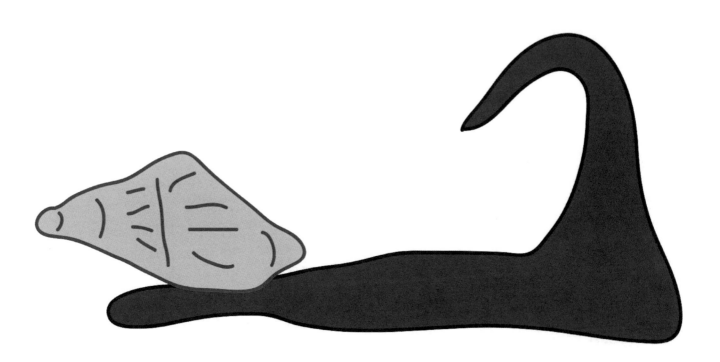

While they are driving, Mikey's thoughts return to the weekend which has just passed.

He remembers that on Sunday, Mommy, Daddy and him went to the beach and played in the ocean.

He also remembers the large seashell he found on the shore and the big crashing waves too.

He loves the ocean!

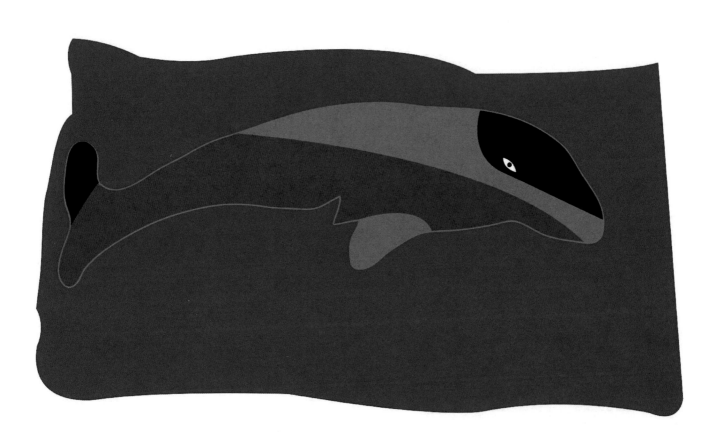

Mikey also remembers that Daddy told him that the ocean is full of many colorful fish and other living animals too.

Daddy said that sometimes big whales swim just below the surface of the water!

Suddenly, Mikey's attention is drawn away from his thoughts about the ocean when he hears the loud siren of a fire truck.

It blazes right by his window on its way to put out a fire!

Mommy and Mikey soon arrive to his school and she parks the car.

Mommy helps Mikey get out of his car seat, and together they gather his lunchbox and water bottle and walk to Mikey's classroom.

When Mikey arrives to his classroom, he sees that his teacher, Miss Sue, is reading the children a story -- about a fish named Wanda.

Mikey gives Mommy a big hug and kiss and says "good-bye" to her.

He joins the other children on the carpet and listens to Miss Sue read the story.

Mikey sees his two good friends, Penny and Jake.

He is excited to play with them, and together they explore their classroom for fun activities to do.

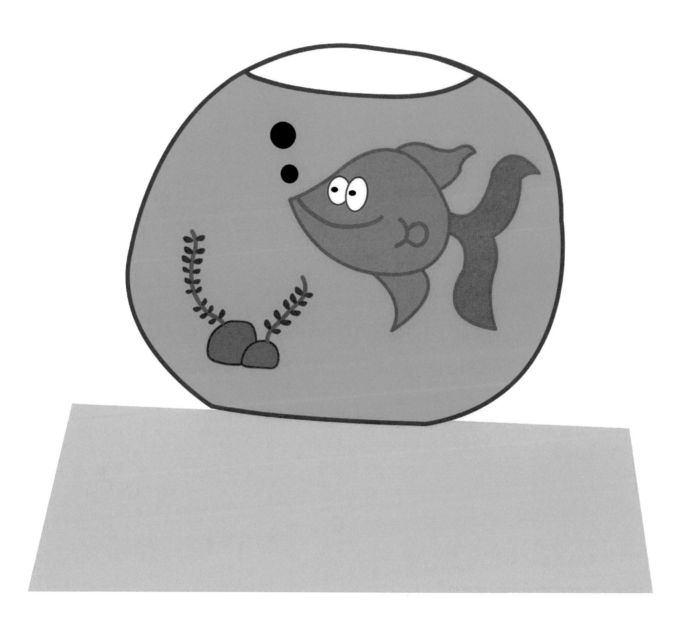

First they visit the class's pet goldfish, Samantha. She is a happy fish and constantly swims around in her fishbowl.

Next they look at the large green dinosaur which is seated on a wooden display table.

Together the class made the dinosaur as a group project. They made it using a material called paper maché, and then took turns painting it.

Miss Sue told them that dinosaurs lived on the Earth *millions of years ago.*

After awhile, Miss Sue announces that it is time for the children to go outside and play on the playground.

Mikey loves to play on the playground, and one of his favorite things to do is to ride the red tricycle.

Mikey enjoys pedaling very fast and racing around the circular path they are allowed to ride in.

Mikey sees his friends Penny and Jake again, and joins them on the slide.

They love climbing up the ladder, and then zooming down the slide as fast as they can!

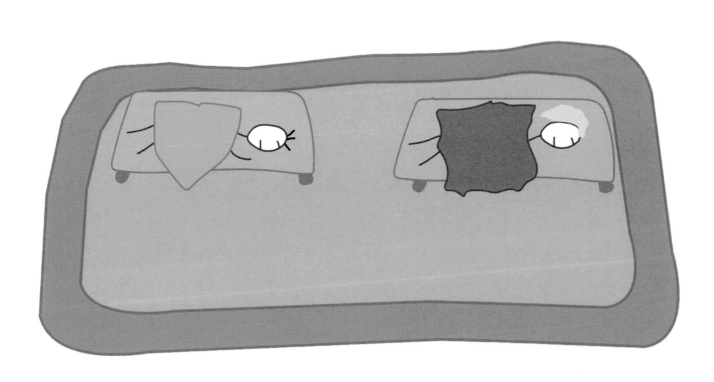

After playing outside for awhile, Mikey and his friends get tired.

Miss Sue calls the children back inside to eat lunch, and then settle down on their cots for nap time.

Mikey enjoys listening to the calm, soothing music Miss Sue plays on the music player – before he drifts off to sleep and into "dreamland".

Soon enough, it is time to wake up from nap time and put their cots away.

The teachers then serve them a yummy snack of celery sticks and hummus.

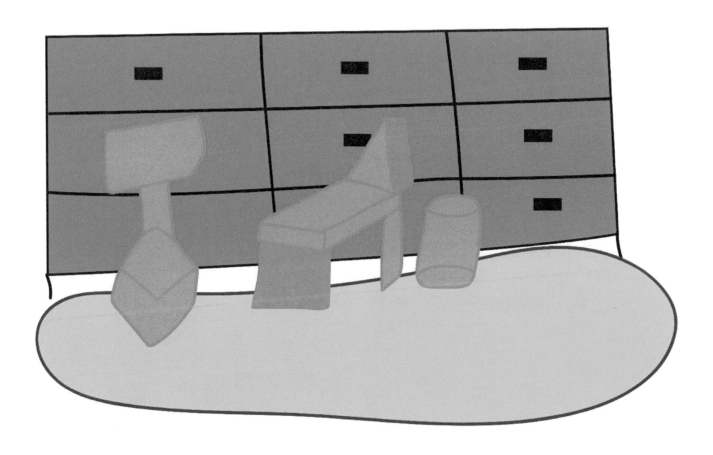

Once again it is free play time, and Mikey chooses to build something with the wooden blocks.

He loves using his imagination to create all sorts of castles, forts and other structures using the wooden blocks.

When he is finished playing with his creations, he enjoys pulling out one of the bottom blocks and watching his structure tumble down into a pile of blocks!

At the end of the day, Mikey feels joyful when Mommy arrives to pick him up and take him home from school.

He always feels great love well up in his heart, and he knows that it will be great to go home to his family after a fun day at school.

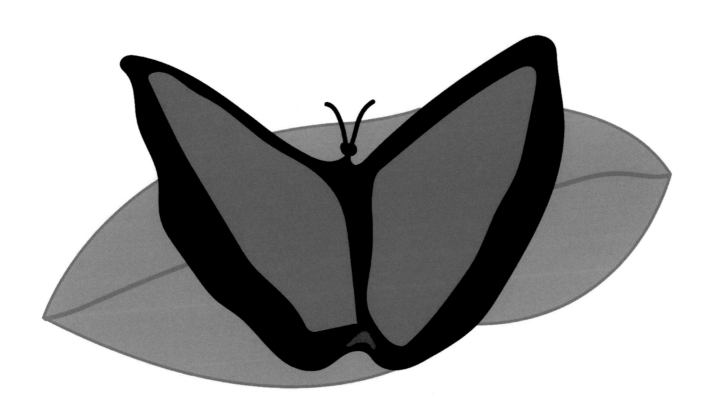

On the drive home from school, Mikey sees a beautiful blue butterfly land on a green leaf.

He remembers what Miss Sue once read to them from a book, that butterflies were once caterpillars before going into a cocoon, and then later re-emerging with wings so that they could fly away.

Soon, Mikey and Mommy arrive to their home.

Mikey feels good, and is happy to be home again in his warm house with Mommy and Daddy.

He had a great day at school!

A Note to Parents and Teachers

The <u>Mikey and Mommy Book Series</u> is intended to be educational for preschool age children. Each book in the series will highlight topics and material related to early childhood development.

In <u>Mikey Goes to School</u>, the below topics and material are introduced in the story:

- ❖ Natural Themes
  - Ocean related – Whales, Seashells, Waves
  - The lifecycle of a Butterfly: Caterpillar, Cocoon and Butterfly
  - Dinosaurs

- ❖ Social/Emotional
  - Parental love
  - Friendship and sharing
  - Group participation

- ❖ Cognitive
  - Memory
  - Imagination
  - Time

Made in the USA
San Bernardino,
CA